If You Ever Get Lost

The Adventures of Julia and Evan

by
Barbara Ann Porte
pictures by Nancy Carpenter

Greenwillow Books
An Imprint of HarperCollins Publishers

If You Ever Get Lost: The Adventures of Julia and Evan
Text copyright © 2000 by Barbara Ann Porte
Illustrations copyright © 2000 by Nancy Carpenter
Printed in the United States of America. For information address
HarperCollins Children's Books, a division of HarperCollins Publishers,
1350 Avenue of the Americas, New York, NY 10019.
http://www.harperchildrens.com

The text of this book is set in Usherwood.

Library of Congress Cataloging-in-Publication Data
Porte, Barbara Ann.
If you ever get lost: the adventures of Julia and Evan /
by Barbara Ann Porte ; illustrated by Nancy Carpenter.
p.   cm.
"Greenwillow Books."
Summary: Julia and her younger brother Evan share several adventures,
including getting lost at a marathon race, going grocery shopping,
helping to catch two thieves at a pet store, and learning to speak Spanish.
ISBN 0-688-16947-3   [1. Brothers and sisters—Fiction.   2. Family life—Fiction.]
I. Carpenter, Nancy, ill.   II. Title.   PZ7.P7995If   2000   [Fic]—dc21
98-32133   CIP   AC

1 2 3 4 5 6 7 8 9 10   First Edition

For my eleven grandchildren—with love
—B.A.P.

For Jen and Veve
—N.C.

Contents

1. If You Ever Get Lost

Julia and Evan, their grandmother and mother, and baby Clarissa are all on their way to the park. The children's father is running in a marathon. They plan to meet him at the finish line.

"Won't Daddy be surprised?" their mother says as they enter the park. "Hold on to each other, and to Grandma or me or the stroller. I don't want anyone getting lost in this crowd. That would be awful!"

She is holding Clarissa now, and also a diaper bag and a backpack of snacks. Grandma is pushing the empty stroller, whose wheels keep getting caught in the grass.

"We should have left the stroller in the van," Grandma grumbles. "Better hurry," she adds. "Getting lost in this crowd would be awful." She herself is hurrying so as not to lose sight of the children's mother, who is walking briskly in front with Clarissa.

"Hold on to me, Evan, and don't let go. There are two zillion three million fourteen hundred and three people here besides us. You don't want to get lost," Julia warns her brother. She is taking giant steps. Evan is jogging, trying hard to keep up.

"Excuse me, Julia, my shoe is untied," Evan says.

Julia sighs and stoops to tie it. "I'm finished," she says finally, standing back up. She squints off into the distance. "I see them," she says. Then, grabbing hold of Evan's hand, she starts off, hurrying.

But when they catch up, they see they've been chasing someone else's mother holding someone else's baby sister. Some girl they've never seen before is pushing that other baby's empty stroller.

"Are we lost, Julia?" Evan asks.

"Of course not," she tells him. "Mommie and Grandma just got ahead. They're probably at the finish line this minute wondering where we are. Don't let go of my hand," Julia warns as she and Evan begin walking again, following the crowd.

"What's that sound?" Evan asks in a while, stretching his neck, dragging his feet. Julia stops and tilts her head to listen.

"We're the fastest, we're the best.

We can run without a rest.

Sound off, one, two.

Sound off, three, four ..."

"Over there," Julia says, pointing. "Those runners are singing a marching song to take their minds off their feet and make themselves forget how tired they are."

Evan nods. Reaching into his jacket pocket, he pulls something out, puts it to his mouth, and blows. It's his harmonica.

"Are we almost there?" he asks after a while.

"Almost. In exactly three minutes and forty-two seconds, we'll be at the finish line," Julia tells him.

Arriving, though, they don't see anyone they know.

"I want Mommie," Evan shouts. "I don't want to be lost."

"Don't cry, Evan," Julia says, seeing a tear. "How can you be lost when you're with me? Look, there's someone who's lost."

Looking, Evan sees a little boy with a red balloon. The
little boy is sobbing.

"Are you lost?" Julia asks him. He nods. "Well, don't

worry. So are our mom and grandma and baby sister, Clarissa. Maybe even our father. You come with us while we find them. They'll know what to do."

Just then Evan begins to tug at Julia's sleeve. "Look, a hot-air balloon," he says, pointing.

Julia looks. At the very top of a very high hill off in the distance, she sees it. She also sees, off to one side, a sound truck. Announcements are being made over a loudspeaker. As far away as they are, though, and amid so much noise, the children can't hear what's being said.

"Follow me," Julia tells both boys. "That must be where they give out the prizes. Mommie, Daddy, Grandma, and Clarissa are probably there this minute, waiting for us to show up. Your mom is probably there, too," she tells the little boy.

"My name is Billy," he says. Holding hands, the three children set out across the field in the direction of the hot-air balloon and the sound truck.

Soon they pass in front of a long table. A teenage girl and

a young man with a ponytail are passing out paper cups of apple juice and doughnuts to the finished runners.

"I'm thirsty," says Evan.

"I'm hungry," says Billy.

Julia feels hungry as a bear herself by now, and just as thirsty. "May we have some?" she asks politely. "We're not actually runners, but my father is."

"Help yourself," says the man. "Most of the runners are through."

The children do. "Thank you," they say.

"You're welcome," says the man.

"You aren't lost, are you?" the teenage girl thinks to call after them.

By the time she does, though, it's too late. They're already out of earshot. And anyway, a small dog is standing directly in front of them, barking. Its leash is being held by a little girl wearing eyeglasses.

"Hi, I'm Gladys. This is my dog, Pip. Have you seen my sisters? They gave me money to buy this T-shirt," she says, holding it out. "They said they'd wait for me right here. Or maybe they said there. Or there."

"Maybe they're waiting for you at the hot-air balloon," Julia suggests helpfully. "That's where they give out prizes and make announcements. We're on our way there now to find our relatives. Do you want to come with us? If you don't see your sisters, our mother will know what to do."

Gladys nods gratefully.

"Take Billy's hand," Julia tells her. Then, seeing a long stick on the ground, Julia picks it up to lean on as she walks.

At last the children are climbing the hill.

"I'm tired, Julia," says Evan.

"I'm tired, too," echoes Billy.

"So are Pip and I," says Gladys.

Julia sighs. If only she could think of a marching song.

Then all of a sudden she does. Waving her stick in the air, she chants loudly:

"We can march and keep the beat.

We have magic in our feet.

Sound off, one, two.

Sound off, three, four."

Billy and Gladys join in, shouting and stamping in time. Evan blows his harmonica. Pip starts to yip at the top of his lungs. It's no wonder the children can't hear the announcements coming from the sound truck.

They pause when they reach the hot-air balloon, where a seated man is pressing a pedal now and then with his foot. With each push comes a loud *whoosh* and a sudden flare as hot air is shot into the balloon.

"That's what keeps it up," Julia explains as Pip and some others jump back in alarm. "Isn't it?" she asks the man. He nods in agreement.

"We'll be right back as soon as we find our relatives," Julia tells him. "Ready, set, go," she says to the others.

Just at that moment, though, a clamor can be heard coming from the direction of the sound truck, and mothers holding babies, and fathers, sisters, and an elderly woman pushing an empty stroller, all come racing toward the children, making so much noise it's hard at first to hear what anyone is saying.

"I thought for sure you'd been kidnapped," Billy's mother keeps telling him.

"Remember, 'Mum's the word' as far as Mom is concerned. No point in worrying her," Gladys's sisters warn her.

"Didn't I tell you to hold on to Grandma or me or the stroller? Then you wouldn't have gotten lost. Until I saw Grandma alone at the finish line looking for us, I thought you were with her." Julia and Evan's mother is trying hard not to raise her voice.

Their grandmother doesn't mind raising hers. "I thought you'd run ahead and caught up with your mother," she says in her loudest tones. "Believe me, when your mother was your age, she listened better."

Julia and Evan are shocked. Isn't anyone happy to see them?

"Well, well, well. All's well that ends well. Isn't that so?"

the children's father booms cheerily. Easy for him to say. Held back in the race by a charley horse in his leg, he'd only limped up the hill himself minutes ago. He hadn't been standing by, frantic, all this time, afraid his missing children might never show up.

As they exit the park, Julia and Evan each hold on to one of his hands. Their grandmother pushes the empty stroller, and their mother carries Clarissa.

"If I've told you once, I've told you a hundred times: If you ever get lost, stay where you are and I will come find you. Why didn't you do that?" she asks.

But before they can answer, they're back at the van.

Julia helps Evan climb in.

"I always thought Mom said if *she* ever got lost, *she* would stand still so we could come find *her*. Isn't that what you thought?" she whispers. Evan nods.

"What's that you say?" asks their grandmother.

"Oh, nothing," Julia replies. Then, softly, under her breath, she starts singing:

"'We can march and keep the beat. We have magic in our feet. . . .' It's a sort of marching song," she adds.

Evan blows a few notes on his harmonica, and baby Clarissa claps. It's a very catchy tune. Soon their father is singing along, and even their grandmother is humming.

"That's quite a concert," says the children's mother, then joins in, whistling as she drives. She sounds just like a piccolo.

The children start to giggle. Soon so does everyone. They sing and giggle, clap and whistle all the way home. Except for Evan, who keeps on blowing.

2. Shopping Excursion

Julia and Evan, their mother, and baby Clarissa are going food shopping.

The children's mom pops Clarissa into the baby compartment of the grocery cart.

"I want to ride, too," says Evan.

"Then where will we put the food?" his mother asks.

"Evan can ride in this cart and I will push him," Julia offers, wheeling over a second, empty one.

"Fine, just don't get lost," their mother says, lifting him in. Has she already forgotten the marathon?

Julia giggles. "You can't get lost in a grocery store. We'll just walk a little ahead and play shopping."

Carefully pushing the cart with Evan in it, she starts down the first aisle. "Potatoes are very nutritious," she says, dropping in a bag of crinkly chips.

Evan reaches for animal crackers.

"Julia, do you think they'll really let us get a dog?" he asks. Both children have begged for one all year.

"When you're old enough to take care of it," their parents have told them.

"Of course. They've already promised. Now they have to," Julia says, steering the cart around the first corner.

"Pet aisle," says Evan.

"That's what I was looking for," Julia tells him. "If we pick out what we need now, by the time our dog comes, we'll be ready. Food first," she says, studying the labels. Then, selecting several cans with pictures of puppies, she hands them to Evan, who lines them up carefully.

"Won't our dog need a bowl to eat from?" Evan asks.

"Right," Julia says, and reaches for a red one.

"Get a blue one for water," Evan tells her. Julia does.

Then, taking turns, they add to the cart: a toy doggie bone, a pink leash and a matching collar with rhinestones, puppy biscuits, vitamins, and a pooper-scooper.

"Is that everything?" Evan asks.

"Almost," says Julia. She's eyeing a row of paperback books. Picking one out, she puts it into the cart.

"So we can read to our puppy?" Evan wants to know.

"So we'll know how to take care of it, how much to feed it, and how to teach it to do tricks."

"But can we still read to it?" Evan asks.

"Of course," Julia says. "We'll start out with *Lassie*."

By now they've come to the end of the aisle. They hear their names being called, and see their mother waving from the end of a long checkout line.

"I was beginning to think you two were lost," she says. Then, looking into their basket, she frowns. "For goodness' sake! What's all that stuff doing in your cart? We'll be here all day just putting it back." Hearing her scold, Clarissa starts to fuss. "Hush now! No one's upset with you," her mother says.

Just at that moment a very tall, frantic-looking woman

with bright red hair comes rushing into the store and up to the counter. She has on a long coat, high boots, a fur hat, and sunglasses.

Through the plate-glass front window, Julia and everyone can see there's a limousine parked outside.

"Please," the woman says to the clerk, "where are your dog things?"

"Dog things, madam?" replies the clerk, who believes everyone should wait her turn regardless of the kind of car she comes in.

"Food, bowls, chains . . ."

"Do you mean leashes?" Julia asks. The woman shifts her gaze down to see who's speaking.

"That, too," she says, then looks at her watch. "Oh, dear, I'm very late. My little boy just won a puppy at the mall. They're both outside in the car with the driver. I've got to get them all back to the nanny right away. 'Don't you bring that puppy home without everything it needs,' the nanny told me on the car phone. 'Not unless you plan to stay and take care of it. There's nothing about puppies in my contract.' Well, I *can't* stay home," says the woman. "I've an important appointment in the city."

While this conversation has been going on, Julia and Evan's mother has been keeping an eye on the slow-moving line. She has important things to do, too. For one, she is hoping to get home in time to feed Clarissa lunch before she falls asleep. With a little luck, maybe Evan will also nap. Counting on her fingers now, the children's mom is wondering how long it will take to put back all the articles in the children's shopping cart.

"Why don't you take our basket?" she hears Julia offer the woman. "There's everything in it a person needs for a puppy."

"Are you sure?" asks the woman. Julia starts naming the items. "I mean, are you sure it's okay if I take them?"

"Oh, yes," Julia tells her. "Our puppy's not even born yet."

For the first time the woman looks in Julia's mother's direction. "Would that be all right?" she asks, sounding confused.

"Please do. In fact, we insist," Julia's mother says.

"This is just so kind of you," says the woman. "What a cute baby," she adds, looking at Clarissa, who is nearly asleep.

Suddenly Clarissa blinks, opens her eyes wide, stares at the woman, and shrieks. You would think she had never seen a redheaded woman in sunglasses before.

"Don't you start that," Clarissa's mother warns, handing her a bottle with juice in it.

Clarissa stops to drink. She watches as the strange lady helps Evan out of the cart, then grabs hold of its handle and pushes off, heading for the counter marked EXPRESS.

By now the children's mother is first in line. She begins unloading her basket. Clarissa, Julia, and Evan all help.

"I bet that boy and his nanny will be glad for the potato chips," Julia whispers to Evan in the parking lot.

"And for the animal crackers, too," says Evan, who wishes he had a lion to munch on this minute.

3. Cloudy with a Chance of Rain

Today is Columbus Day, so there isn't any school. Julia and Evan are just finishing lunch when a long package arrives in the mail addressed to them. It's from their aunt Quincy.

"Can we open it?" the children ask.

"Go ahead," says their mother. Then she lifts Clarissa out of her high chair and carries her off for a nap.

Julia and Evan unwrap the box. Inside are presents for them: two umbrellas. One has black Scottie dogs printed all around it. The other has yellow giraffes.

"Which one do you want, Evan?" Julia asks. Evan looks at

them both, trying to decide. Julia's already made up her mind. "You like dogs. Why don't you pick that one?" she says. Now both children have the umbrellas they want.

"I wish it were raining," says Evan.

"There's a cloud," Julia says, pointing at the window.

"Let's open our umbrellas and practice using them inside."
So they do. They walk back and forth in the living room,
umbrellas up, pretending it's a rainy day.

"Sun's out!" Julia says. Setting her open umbrella in the
middle of the floor, she crawls under it. "Don't you just love
a sandy beach? Here, take this money and go buy us soda
pops, French fries, and hot dogs. I want mine with ketchup,
mustard, sauerkraut, onions, relish, and salsa."

"From where?" Evan asks, holding out his hand. His own
umbrella lies open on the floor in the corner where he
plopped it.

Julia points at it. "See that stand with all the dogs on it?"
she says.

When Evan gets back with the food, the children have a
picnic.

"Can we go swimming?" Evan asks in a while.

"It's too soon after eating. We can go for a parachute
ride," Julia tells him.

Holding up her umbrella, she climbs on a chair, then

jumps off it. Holding up his umbrella, Evan climbs on a different chair, then jumps off it. Then Julia jumps, then Evan, then Julia, then Evan.

"What are you children doing in there?" their mother calls from the bedroom. "Stop all that noise before you wake up Clarissa."

"Fine. We'll do something quiet," says Julia. But what? Then she knows.

She drags the two chairs to opposite ends of the room. Taking a long piece of string from a drawer, she lays it in a straight line between them on the floor. "Tightrope walking doesn't make noise. Lend me your parasol, please," she whispers to Evan.

Now, holding one umbrella in each hand for balance, Julia steps along the string, placing one foot in front of the other very carefully so as not to fall off. She does a few tricks when she gets to the middle—stands on one leg, takes several hops. When she comes to the far chair, she climbs on it, takes her bows, and climbs off.

"Is it my turn now?" Evan asks.

"Yes, but be careful. If you fall, you could break something."

Step by step, Evan crosses the tightrope carefully, stopping only in the middle to do a few tricks. When he comes to the end, he climbs on the chair and takes his bows.

"What can we do now?" he asks.

"You can close those nice new umbrellas," their mother says, passing through the room, a stack of laundry in her arms. "It isn't raining in the house."

Julia closes hers, then helps Evan close his.

"Hurry! Quick! Get behind me! Keep in line and march. It's a parade," Julia tells him.

Waving her baton like a drum major, Julia struts around in the living room with Evan right behind. With every other step he takes, he taps his umbrella on the floor. He also drags one leg.

"What are you doing?" Julia asks.

"I sprained my ankle on the high wire. That's why I'm using a cane," he replies.

"I see," their mother says, having returned, ready now to admire the presents.

"Can we play outside?" Julia asks.

"It's starting to rain," her mother answers, looking through a window.

"Good! We can use our umbrellas. Can we?" asks Evan.

"Fine. Just try not to get wet," says his mother.

So the children put on their rain slickers, rain hats, and boots, take their umbrellas, and go outside. They walk up and down on the sidewalk in front of their house.

Soon Julia is walking on tiptoes and bobbing her head. "Look at me, Evan! I'm an umbrella bird from Brazil," she says.

"I'm an umbrella bird, too," says Evan, doing the same.

Watching through the window, their mother calls to them to come in. "You looked so cold out there," she tells them, as she heats milk for cocoa and puts out cookies.

After they've finished their snacks, the children write a thank-you letter to Aunt Quincy. Their mother helps them address it and puts on a stamp. By then Clarissa's awake and the rain has stopped.

"Let's go for a walk," their mother says, and puts Clarissa into the stroller. She also packs a bottle of juice.

Evan and Julia pack their umbrellas. "In case there's a change in the weather," says Julia.

They all three take turns pushing the stroller. They walk as far as the mailbox and drop in the letter. On the way home it starts to drizzle.

"It's a good thing this stroller has a hood," their mother says, raising it.

"It's a good thing we have umbrellas," Julia and Evan say, opening theirs and holding them up.

4. Counting

Julia and Evan are helping their mother bake brownies. "How many brownies are we making?" Evan asks.

"How many do we need?" his mother answers.

Evan counts on his fingers: "Joe, Marie, Charlie, Eduardo, Edwina, and me. That's six. Do we need six?" Tomorrow Evan's play group is meeting at his house.

"What if some of your friends want more than one? And maybe some of their moms like brownies, too. Don't you think we should offer one to each mom before she goes home?" (Pay attention now. This isn't a story for ninnies to follow.)

Evan counts again. Running out of fingers, he borrows some of Julia's. He counts two for each child and one for each mother. Eduardo and Edwina, being twins, have only one mother between them.

"How many are there now?" Evan asks, confused by so many fingers.

"If there are six children, and each child eats two, that's twelve brownies," Julia informs him. "There are four mothers plus ours. That makes five more to count: thirteen, fourteen, fifteen, sixteen, seventeen. It's called adding," Julia says, shaking out her fingers.

"We need seventeen brownies," Evan tells his mother.

"Are you sure?" his mother asks. "Are you absolutely positive? What about Julia? Maybe Daddy will want one."

"What about Clarissa?" Evan asks.

"Babies can't eat brownies," Julia points out.

"So how many do we need?" asks Evan, tired of counting.

Julia's also tired. She turns to their mother for help, but first reminds her, "Don't forget, children get two."

"Right," says her mother, then adds three more to the total, two for Julia and one for her father: "Eighteen, nineteen, twenty."

"Is that how many brownies we're making, twenty?" asks Evan.

"I think twenty-four; that way we'll be certain of having more than enough," his mother replies.

"What will we do with the extras?" asks Julia.

"Let's not be like the farmer who counted the chickens before they were hatched. I suggest we bake our brownies first, then decide," says her mother.

That's what they do.

When the baking pan comes from the oven, the children sniff, and eye it with pleasure.

Their mother sets it to cool on a wire rack. Carefully she cuts the cake into perfect squares. "There, that's two dozen," she says.

Julia knows a dozen is twelve; twelve and twelve is

twenty-four. Julia counts them all to be sure. Then she
counts once more and stops at twenty.

"I think whoever cleans her plate best at dinner should
get the extra four. Is that what you think?" she asks her
mother.

"We'll see," says her mother.

Julia closes her eyes and does arithmetic in her head. If
she and Evan *both* clean their plates, that would be two
brownies each for dessert. Opening her eyes, Julia looks at

her brother. He's such a picky eater. Still, four would be a lot for her to eat by herself. Maybe she'll eat two tonight and take the other two with her to school tomorrow. She'll give one to her best friend, Carmen, at lunch. That way she'll still have her own original two for an after-school snack. Just thinking about it makes her mouth water.

"Guess what?" Evan says, interrupting Julia's thoughts.

"What?" says his mother.

"I counted twenty-four brownies. You said we needed twenty. That means we have four left over. If Julia and I and you and Daddy all clean our plates at dinner, there will be one brownie for each of us for dessert."

Julia sighs. She sees her brother is right. "Evan's smart for his age, isn't he?" she asks their mother.

"All my children are smart," says her mother. She hugs them both, then serves them each a brownie. "It's a special treat for helping me bake."

"Ummmm," says Evan, eating slowly to make his last. "Dessert tastes better before dinner, doesn't it?" he asks.

"That's because it's still warm," Julia tells him, finished with hers.

Already she's counting on her fingers how many brownies might be left tomorrow after Evan's play group meets. What if some children want only one? What if some moms don't want any? There could be a lot.

5. Bicycle Lesson

Julia and Evan, their mother and father, and baby Clarissa are getting ready to leave for the park.

"You may each take one possession," their mother tells Julia and Evan.

Julia decides on her bicycle, and Evan picks Bill, his toy monkey.

"Are you sure you wouldn't rather take your bicycle? The park is a good place to practice riding," his mother tells him. Evan's bicycle is brand-new, shiny blue with training wheels.

Evan shakes his head.

"He doesn't like pedaling," Julia explains.

"I see," says their mother. She hopes he doesn't change his mind when they get there.

Of course he does.

"I want my bicycle, too," Evan says, seeing zillions of bicyclists speeding by.

"I was afraid that would happen," says his mother.

"He can borrow mine," Julia offers kindly. "I'll watch Bill while you practice riding," she tells her brother. "Remember, though, I don't have training wheels."

"I know," he says.

Then, placing her helmet on his head, Julia helps Evan climb on. He starts to pedal. Julia holds on to the seat and runs alongside to help him balance. Pretty soon she starts to get tired. She lets go of the seat.

Evan wobbles, then straightens, wobbles, then straightens, finally falls. He picks himself up, climbs back on, and pedals some more.

"Look at Evan! He's riding by himself," Julia calls to their parents. They are seated on a park bench, taking turns rocking Clarissa back and forth in her stroller.

"Good for you, Evan," his parents call by way of encouragement.

Sitting in the shade of a tree now, catching her breath,

Julia cuddles the monkey. "I knew he could do it. It just takes practice," she tells it.

Pleased by his progress, Evan keeps practicing. He pedals, then falls, pedals, then falls, pedals, then falls. Then suddenly he is pedaling and pedaling.

"Look at me," he shouts. "I can ride by myself!"

"Be careful," his parents warn. "That's far enough. Come back," they call.

But Evan, concentrating so hard on keeping his balance, doesn't hear them.

Suddenly the path he's on begins to wind and to run downhill. Evan sees that at the bottom there's a pond. Some children are riding bicycles around it. Some are roller-skating. Others are sailing toy boats.

Evan is picking up speed. There's a breeze on his face. He's almost flying. Then, ever so faintly, he hears his name being called.

"Evan, stop! Come back! Mommie and Daddy said you're going too far." It's Julia, chasing after him, shouting.

Frightened by now, Evan would like to stop but doesn't know how. He hasn't the least idea. Not a clue. He'd like to turn around and ask Julia, but it's taking all his attention just to keep his front wheel straight. He's going too fast to try dragging his feet on the ground. He's afraid he'll get hurt if he falls.

At that same moment, it occurs to Julia that she never showed her brother how to brake. "Press back on the pedals! Press back on the pedals!" she yells.

But Evan's too far away to hear what she's saying. Julia is running as fast as she can, but she's no match for a bicycle racing downhill.

Then suddenly Evan stops being afraid. He starts to feel better. Not just better. He starts to feel fine. He sees that all around the pond is a rim, a raised border, sort of a bumper. Children are leaning over it to put their toy boats in the water.

Of course! It's there to keep people from falling in, Evan tells himself. When this bicycle hits that rim, it's sure to stop. Then I'll climb off. Won't everyone be surprised at how well I can ride!

By now, not only Julia but also her parents are running down the hill, along with Clarissa, who is clapping her hands and shrieking gleefully. It's the fastest she has ever ridden in her stroller.

"Evan, please stop," Julia is calling. If she were not hurrying so, she'd be crying. She's that upset.

"Somebody please stop that child," Evan's father is shouting.

"No, no, no, no. Please don't let anything bad happen," Evan's mother is saying, though it's not clear to whom.

Just then Evan reaches the bottom of the hill. With the bicycle well balanced and its front wheel straight, Evan is bravely heading toward the water.

"Stop, bicycle!" he tells it in that second before its wheel hits the rim.

But the bicycle doesn't. As far as those watching can tell,

it doesn't even slow down. Up and over the rim it goes, with Evan still on it.

A young man, sitting on a bench studying, hears the splash and looks up. At once he's in the water, lifting Evan out. Setting him spluttering on the ground alongside the pond, the student pats him on his back.

By this time Evan's family has caught up to him, all of them breathless, except for Clarissa. Bystanders have clustered in a crowd. Someone hands Evan's father a blanket to wrap Evan in. Someone else hands Evan a hot dog and a soda pop, bought from a nearby stand.

"That was a close call. What a brave little boy you are," strangers are telling him. Julia doesn't see why. She thinks if anyone was brave, it's the man who went to Evan's rescue.

He is back in the water right now, thigh deep, pulling out her bicycle, for which she is grateful. He wipes it dry with his jacket.

"We can't thank you enough," Julia's father says, having handed Evan over to his mother. As Julia takes charge of her bicycle, her father tries to hand the young man some paper money, but he won't take it.

"Oh, no. I'm just glad I was here and could help," the young man insists.

"Please keep it," says Evan's mother. She's holding Evan tightly in her arms. He's licking mustard off his hot dog. "Your clothes will need cleaning, your sneakers are ruined, even your book's gotten damp."

That's certainly true. The student's clothes and sneakers, in fact, are not only wet but covered with brown slime and green algae from the pond. So is the student.

"Dry off and go home," the children's mother tells him. "Take a warm shower. Have some hot soup. I'd feel awful thinking you'd caught a chill."

The student decides to take her advice. "Thank you," he says. He pats Evan's head before leaving.

"What about me?" Julia mutters under her breath, watching him go. How she hates feeling left out. So what if she didn't land in the pond? Isn't she covered in sweat from all that running? And isn't it her bicycle, after all, that got wet? Besides which, she's hungry.

That's when she feels a tap on her shoulder. It's her father, holding out two ice-cream cups.

"Take one," he says. He shares the other with Clarissa.

"Thank you," says Julia. "Bill misses you," she tells Evan, and hands him the monkey she's been clutching all this time. Then, in between spoonfuls of ice cream, she gives her brother a bicycle lesson: "Stopping is easy," she tells him. "You only need to press back with your feet on the pedals. Remember to do that next time."

"Yes," Evan says. "Next time I will."

6. A Scary Story

"**D**o you want to hear a scary story?" Julia asks Evan. Evan does. "It's really true, too. I'm not making it up," Julia says, and begins.

"There are furry creatures living in our attic. They have beady yellow eyes, pointy ears, sharp teeth, long skinny tails, and feet with claws. They look a little like weasels, but with red curly hair. There used to be only two, but now there are hundreds."

"There are not, either," says Evan.

"Are, too. Ssssh! Listen. What do you hear?" Julia asks.

"Noises," says Evan, listening. "Tick, tock, tink—plinkity-plink, sounds like that."

"See, that's what I'm telling you," says his sister. "It's the furry creatures in the attic that are making all that noise."

"What do they eat?" Evan asks.

"Whatever they find," Julia answers. "Insects, spiders, squirrels, pigeons, now and then a roof rat. That's what they like the best. The furry creatures reach their claws through the air vents and catch them. Do you want to know what else they eat?" Julia asks.

"What?" says Evan.

"Well, I know it's really disgusting, but when they can't find anything else to eat, they sometimes eat one another." Julia shudders just thinking about it.

Evan shudders, too. "But it's not true," he says. Then he asks, "What do they drink?"

"Rainwater," answers Julia. "In the winter, melted snow. It's a good thing, too, that they do. Otherwise it would leak through the ceiling and make everything wet. Remember what happened next door after last winter's blizzard, how water dripped down through the Jacksons' chandelier onto their table and ruined it, the carpet, the floor, and three of their dining-room chairs?"

Evan nods, remembering. "What would happen if the furry creatures got out and came down?" he asks.

"Ooooh, that would be awful," says Julia, and covers her eyes. "They'd gobble our food, chew on our furniture, tear up our clothing, take over our beds. Probably they'd bite us, besides." Her eyes uncovered now, and open wide, Julia shudders again.

"It isn't even true," says Evan.

"Is, too," says Julia.

"I'm asking Mom," Evan says, and stomps off to find her.

"Julia says there are red furry creatures living in our attic. Are there?" Evan asks when he does.

"Of course not," she tells him.

"That's what I told Julia," says Evan.

"Well, you were right," says his mother.

"But what if there were?" he asks.

"I'd sprinkle mothballs. Mothballs keep everything away. Besides, your father was in the attic last Sunday looking for his old baseball glove. If any furry creatures were up there, believe me, he would have told me."

Evan is glad to hear it.

Getting into bed that night, he tells his monkey, Bill, "It's just a stupid story old Julia made up."

Julia, that moment, is standing in her walk-in closet, putting on her pajamas. Looking up, she sees a large square cut into the ceiling, with a wooden frame around it. It looks a lot like a window, lying flat, with a paper pane. She points it out to her mother. "What's that?" she asks.

"An access door," her mother tells her. "You need a ladder, and then you can climb through it into the attic."

"Have you ever?" Julia asks.

"No, but Daddy has. He stores some of his old things in boxes up there."

"Oh," Julia says, and wonders that she never noticed it before.

In bed she whispers to her imaginary friend, Bettina, "See, the part about the attic is true, but I made up all the rest. There are no furry creatures up there."

Then, lying very still in the dark, Julia hears something: a sort of swooshing, whooshing noise. She pulls her blanket over her head. "It's probably just the wind," she tells Bettina. But now there comes a rapping, tapping sound—a plinking sort of noise. "Seeds," Julia murmurs. "They're falling from the trees onto the roof. The wind must be blowing them down."

For the next instant everything's quiet. Then the rapping and tapping begin again and get louder. Somewhere above her Julia hears scratching.

Sure what it is now, she sits up and starts shrieking, "They're coming! They're coming! They're trying to get in!"

Her parents come running. They turn on a light. "What is it? What's wrong?"

Wide awake now, and startled by so much noise, Evan, too, rushes to see. "It could be furry creatures," he tells his monkey. "Or else Julia's having a bad dream." Reaching her doorway, he halts and looks in.

She's stopped shrieking by now and is gasping for air. In between gasps, she's trying to speak. Something to do with yellow teeth, curly tails, sharp red claws, and long pointy feet.

"Take a deep breath and relax," her mother says. "I can't understand a word that you're saying."

Julia breathes deeply, then tries again.

"They're coming! They're coming! They're trying to get in," she wails, this time pointing toward her closet ceiling.

"Julia thinks there are red furry creatures living in the attic," Evan explains. "She probably dreamed they were coming down to bite her. I told her it was only a stupid story she made up, but she wouldn't believe me."

"I see," says their mother.

"But it's really true," Julia whispers. "Listen!"

Everyone does, except for Clarissa, who's still asleep in her crib. How can she sleep through so much commotion?

"That's the heating system you hear. It's the noise made by hot air when it blows through the ducts in the walls," Julia's father tells her.

They listen some more.

"That's the refrigerator motor humming," her mother says. "It's making ice cubes now," she adds as they hear a clunking sound.

"I think I hear squirrels walking on the roof," says Evan.

"How come I never heard all this before?" Julia asks.

"You did. You just weren't paying attention," her mother answers.

"Now, both of you, please go to sleep," says their father.

Then he and their mother kiss the children good night, turn off the light, and go downstairs. Evan heads for his room.

"I guess I never paid attention before, either," he tells Bill. "Or possibly the furry creatures were making too much noise for me to hear," he adds, tucking both himself and Bill in. "Pleasant dreams and sleep tight," he whispers.

Meantime, Julia has gotten up from her bed, closed her closet door tightly, and dragged a chair in front of it. "Of course I know there's nothing there. It was a story I made up," she tells Bettina, snuggling down beside her in bed. "Still, it never hurts to be sure."

7. Nature Study

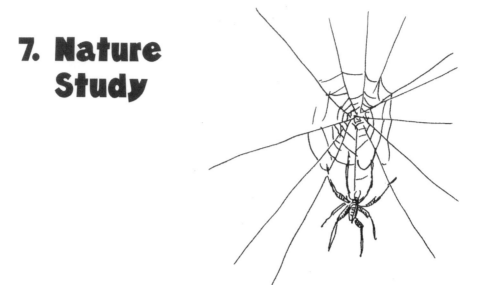

Why are Julia and Evan sitting on the floor staring up through the glass panes of their grandmother's front door, pinching themselves to stay awake? It's barely morning. The sun isn't even up yet. Except for the porch light and the half moon still visible in the sky, it's dark outside. What can they be watching for?

"Stay awake! If you close your eyes, you'll miss it. I've missed it plenty of times myself," the children's grandmother warns them.

Julia and Evan are visiting this week, sleeping in the bunk beds in the extra bedroom. Clarissa's still a baby, so they left her at home.

"Evan's asleep," Julia announces. She tickles the bottoms of his feet to wake him.

"I am not. I was only resting my eyes," he replies. Outside it is just starting to get light.

"Don't even blink," their grandmother says. "Remember, it doesn't do it every day. It may not do it today. But once it starts, it's over in a minute."

Julia and Evan know that it's true. This is their third morning trying not to miss it. They fell asleep on the floor the other two. Their grandmother sits down beside them now to keep them awake.

See all three sitting on the floor, staring hard toward the light coming in at the door? Clearly visible through the glass is a very large, very round, nearly perfect spider's web. And head down, dead center at its hub, still as anything, waits the spider that made it. All August long, that spider's been there every night, like this, on guard.

Sleepy, Julia nods.

Evan nudges her. "Wake up!" he says.

"I'm up!" she answers.

Then just at that moment, what they have been waiting three days to see, watching for almost an hour this morning, begins.

The spider starts moving. Racing to the top of its web, it stuffs silk into its mouth as it goes, leaving nothing behind it. Then crisscrossing the web in what looks like a frenzy, it takes down in seconds what took it, the evening before, two hours to build. At last only space remains where before was a web. One last silk thread, invisibly tacked, rises to the topmost, right-hand corner of the entranceway.

By now the children and their grandmother are on their feet, three faces pressed to the glass. They watch as the spider goes up that final strand.

In slow motion, pulled along only by its front pairs of
legs, it seems to glide, gathering the silk as it climbs, until
finally all that remains is a tiny black speck, like a piece of

dust—the spider tucked up asleep beneath the entranceway eaves. There it will stay until evening, when it will come down again to start weaving.

"Wow!" says Julia.

"If you didn't know it was there, you wouldn't know it was there, would you?" Evan says, his eyes still glued to that spot.

"Say what?" asks the children's grandmother. She's already in the kitchen, running water, rattling pots, getting ready to fix breakfast.

8. Speaking Spanish

"*Buenos días,*" Julia tells Evan and her mother, getting off the school bus. "*Buenos días,*" she says to Clarissa, who is waving from her stroller.

It is the first week of school, and Julia is in the Spanish immersion class. Evan is in kindergarten now, but that's only in the mornings.

"*Buenos días,*" says their mother, kissing Julia hello.

"Do you know what Julia is saying?" Evan mutters to his truck. "I don't know what she is saying."

Ever since they started school this fall, Evan thinks that Julia has been acting funny. He doesn't mean funny ha-ha. He means funny strange. He wishes she'd go back to speaking plain English.

Inside, the children's mother pours cold milk into tall glasses and sets a plate of ginger snaps at the table.

"*La leche es buena,*" says Julia. "So are the cookies. *Gracias, Mamá.*"

"May I please be excused?" Evan asks, pushing back his glass.

"Yes, just don't spill that milk," warns his mother, busy with Clarissa.

Evan goes into the family room and lies down on the floor. He wraps his blanket around his ears. Even so he keeps hearing what Julia is saying.

"*Señorita Fernández* says our class is doing very well. She says she can hardly believe how much Spanish we've learned in just our first week. Well, I think she doesn't mean Ronald Alperstein. He was so bad at snack time today,

Señorita Fernández had to stop speaking in Spanish and yell at him in English."

Good old Ronald Alperstein, thinks Evan.

At dinner that night Evan's father looks at him and asks, "So, how was school today?"

"Fine," Evan answers. "I like kindergarten."

"Don't you want to know how my school was?" Julia asks.

"Of course I do. How was your school?" asks her father.

"*Bien,*" says Julia. "*Muy bien.* That means very good."

"*Muy bien,*" says her father. "*Me alegro.* That means I'm glad."

"You can speak Spanish?" Julia asks, surprised.

"*Un poco,*" her father replies. "A little. I took it in high school, but I've hardly had a chance to use it since."

"Did you take Spanish in high school, too?" Julia asks her mother.

"French," says her mother. "*Parlez-vous Français?*"

"What else can you say?" Julia asks.

"Not much," her mother answers. "No one I knew spoke French for me to practice with. Too bad I didn't take Yiddish. Then I could have practiced with my mother."

"Grandma speaks Yiddish?" Evan asks.

"Used to. She used to speak it with *her* mother. In those days, though, they called it speaking Jewish. Grown-ups used it when they didn't want the children to know what they were saying."

"What were they saying?" Julia asks.

"How would I know?" her mother answers. "They said it in Yiddish."

"See," Julia tells Evan a little while later. They're both in the bathroom getting ready for bed.

"See what?" he asks.

"If you take Spanish immersion next year, too, we can practice together. That way we'll never forget. Plus, we can speak to each other in Spanish when we don't want the grown-ups to know what we're saying."

Busy brushing his teeth, his mouth running over with paste, Evan doesn't answer.

"*Buenas noches,*" Julia tells him, all washed and brushed herself now. "It means good-night," she calls back, leaving the room.

Evan puts down his brush and inspects his teeth. He spits into the sink, then rinses. *"Buenas noches, buenas noches, buenas noches,"* he mouths at the mirror. Then, jumping down from his stepstool, he heads for the hall.

He tiptoes into Clarissa's room. She's sound asleep in her crib. He pats her gently on the head, then practices: *"Buenas*

noches, Clarissa," he whispers. "Pleasant dreams and sleep tight."

Back in the hallway again, he stops outside Julia's door. "*Buenas noches,* Julia," he whispers once more. "Pleasant dreams and sleep tight."

Then he enters his own room. His monkey, Bill, is already in bed. "*Buenas noches,* Bill," Evan says, climbing in beside him. "Pleasant dreams and sleep tight."

He plans to ask Julia, in the morning, how to say the English part in Spanish.

9. Pet Store Holdup

It's Saturday morning. Julia, Evan, and their father have been busy running errands. On their way home, they see a sign: EXOTIC PET STORE, it reads. Their father parks the car. All three go inside. Everywhere are tanks and cages. They house snakes and lizards, frogs and toads, turtles, salamanders, also talking parrots, ferrets, and chinchillas.

"I'll wait for you here by the cricket tank," their father says.

Julia goes off to talk with a parrot.

Evan heads for the snake department. Two customers are already there. One of them is wearing a blue cap and a gray sweatshirt with writing. The other has on a red cap and a yellow sweatshirt with writing. Evan watches them carefully as they make up their minds which snakes to buy. Finally they decide.

"We'll take that pair," they tell the owner, who uses a forked stick to transfer the snakes from their pet-store home into a carrying case. Then the owner helps his customers select a tank in which to keep their snakes.

"You'll want some white mice, too, to feed them," the owner says, and adds four to the order. Arranging everything inside the tank, he carries it to the cash register at the front of the store.

Hoping to find out how much a pair of snakes costs, Evan follows. He watches as the owner rings up the sale. Then, just as the two men seem about to pay for their purchase, they grab the tank instead, with everything in it, and race out the door.

Evan can hardly believe his eyes. Those two men weren't customers at all. They're robbers. Evan has never seen robbers before.

"Hey, come back! Stop, thieves!" the store owner shouts, rushing after them. He calls over his shoulder to the children's father, "Please—will you watch the cash register for me?"

Of course the children's father does. But before he can sell even one thing, the owner returns, perspiring and out of breath from so much running. Still gasping for air, he reports on what happened: Unfortunately he didn't catch the thieves. Fortunately he did get a good look at their getaway car, which was bright red, and also at the first three letters on their license plate. Then, just after the thieves had driven off, a policewoman came along. The store owner gave her a full report, after which he ran all the way back to the store.

"I certainly hope they catch those thieves," the children's father tells the owner, shepherding Julia and Evan toward the door. He is anxious now to be on his way. By this time, his wife must be wondering where they all are. Perhaps he's worried, too, that the thieves will come back, or else some others.

"Thank you," says the owner, and shrugs. That the thieves will get caught seems unlikely to him.

At that moment, though, the telephone rings. It's the policewoman calling. She's apprehended two suspects traveling in a bright red car with a pair of snakes in a carrying case, four white mice, and a glass tank. The license plate letters match the store owner's report. Does the owner recall what the thieves were wearing?

"What they were wearing?" the owner echoes, and scratches his head. Regarding their dress, his mind is a blank.

"I remember," says Evan. "One of them was wearing a blue cap and a gray sweatshirt with writing. The other had on a red cap and a yellow sweatshirt with writing."

So do the two men in the car. The policewoman now tells the owner she needs him to come to where she is and make a positive identification so that she can hold the suspects.

Hearing this, how surprised everyone is.

"Wouldn't you think two men in the right clothes, in a red car with a pair of snakes, four white mice, a glass tank, and the right license plate would be sufficient?" says the children's father.

"Oh, well," says the store owner, picking up a ring of keys. "I suppose I'd have to go there anyway to get back my snakes. Thank you for looking after my store," he tells Julia and Evan's father. "Come back another time," he tells them all.

"Oh, we will," they say. They shake the owner's hand and leave. The owner follows them out and locks the door.

"Did you have a nice morning?" the children's mother asks when they get home.

"Oh, yes," the children answer.

"Sorry we're so late. We got held up in a pet store," their father says. "Wait until you hear what happened."

Then, taking turns, they tell her.